RIKI LEVINSON

Watch the Stars Come Out

ILLUSTRATED BY DIANE GOODE

ORCHARD BOOKS · LONDON

Text copyright © 1985 by Riki Friedberg Levinson
Illustrations copyright © 1985 by Diane Goode
First published in the United States by E. P. Dutton 1985
First published in Great Britain 1986 by

ORCHARD BOOKS

10 Golden Square, London WIR 3AF
14 Mars Road, Lane Cove NSW 2066

ISBN 1 85213 001 6

Printed in Hong Kong by South China Printing Co

for my Mort and Gerry—
remembering Anna, my Mama
R.L.

to Peter Goode
D.G.

Grandma told me when her Mama was a little
girl she had red hair—just like me.

Grandma's Mama loved to go to bed early and
watch the stars come out—just like me.

Every Friday night, after the dishes were put
away, Grandma's Mama would come to her room
and tell her a special story.

When I was a little girl, my big Brother and I
went on a big boat to America. Mama and Papa
and Sister were waiting there for us.

My aunt, Mama's sister, took us to the boat.
She didn't bring my two little brothers. They
were too small. They would come on a boat
when they were older.

Aunt gave us a barrel full of dried fruit. She
asked an old lady to watch over us. And she did.
She also ate our dried fruit.

The old lady and Brother and I went down the steps to our room. I counted the steps as we carried our bundles down, but there were so many, I forgot to count after a while.

Sometimes the boat rocked back and forth—it was
fun! Some people didn't like it—they got sick. The
old lady got very, very sick. She died.

Brother told me not to worry. He would take care
of me—he was ten.

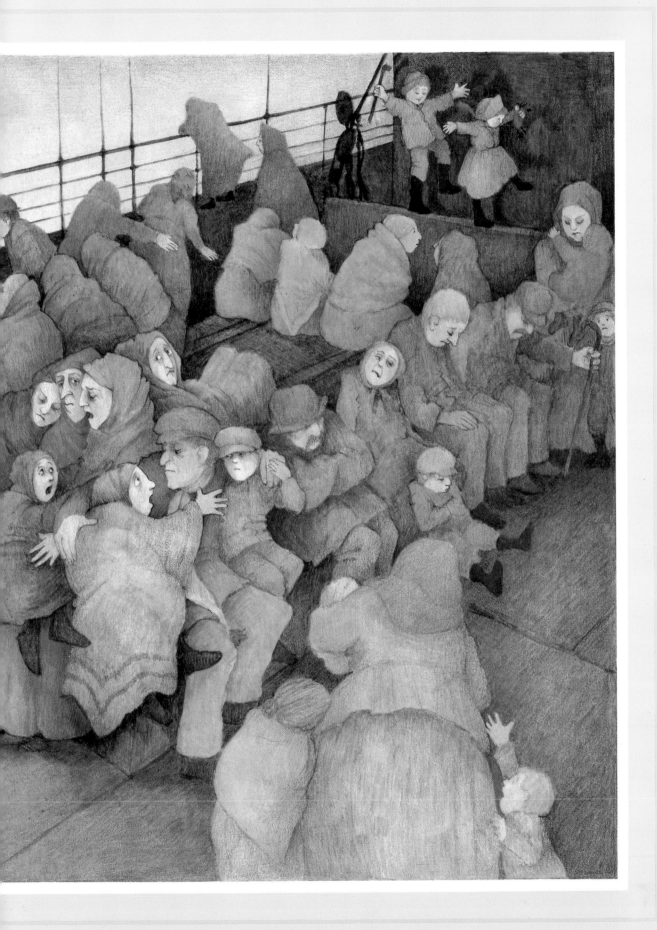

At night when I went to sleep, I couldn't see
the stars come out in the sky. That made me sad.

Each morning when we got up, Brother put a mark on his stick. I counted them—twenty-three.

The last morning we looked across the water. There were two islands near each other. One of them had a statue standing on it—a lady with a crown. Everyone got very excited and waved to her. I did too.

When the boat stopped, we carried our bundles down the plank.

I started to cry. I did not see Mama and Papa and Sister. A sailor told me not to worry—we would see them soon.

We went on another boat to a place on an island.

We carried our bundles into a big, big room.
Brother and I went into a small room with all
the other children without mamas and papas.
A lady looked at me all over. I wondered why.
I waited for Brother. The lady looked at him too.

The next day we went on a ferry. The land came
closer and closer as we watched. Everyone waved.
We did too.

Mama and Papa and Sister were there!

We went on a trolley to our home. Mama said
it was a palace.
Mama's palace was on the top floor. I counted
the steps as we walked up—fifty-two!

Mama and Papa's room was in the middle. Our room was in the front. And in the back was the kitchen with a big black stove.

Mama warmed a big pot of water on the stove. She poured some into the sink and helped me climb in to wash.

Mama washed my hair, and when it was dry,
she brushed it. It felt good.
Sister gave us cookies and glasses of tea.
I was very tired.

I kissed Mama and Sister good-night. Papa patted me on my head and said I was his little princess.

I went into our room and climbed into Sister's bed. It was right next to the window.

I watched the stars come out. One, two, three.

This Friday night I will go to bed very early
and watch the stars come out in the sky.
  I hope Grandma will come to my room and
tell me another special story.